GAME OVER

LOADING...
LOADING...
LOADING...

NO SIGNAL

HELLO! hello!

Matthew Cordell

Disney • HYPERION BOOKS • New York

Hello, Mom.

Hello.

Hello, Dad.

Hello.

Hello, Bob.

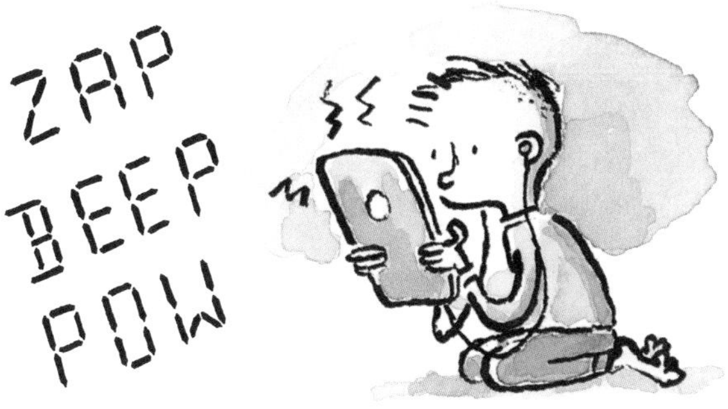
ZAP
BEEP
POW

Sigh.

Hmmm...

Hello...

...leaf.

Hello, bug.

Hello,

flower.

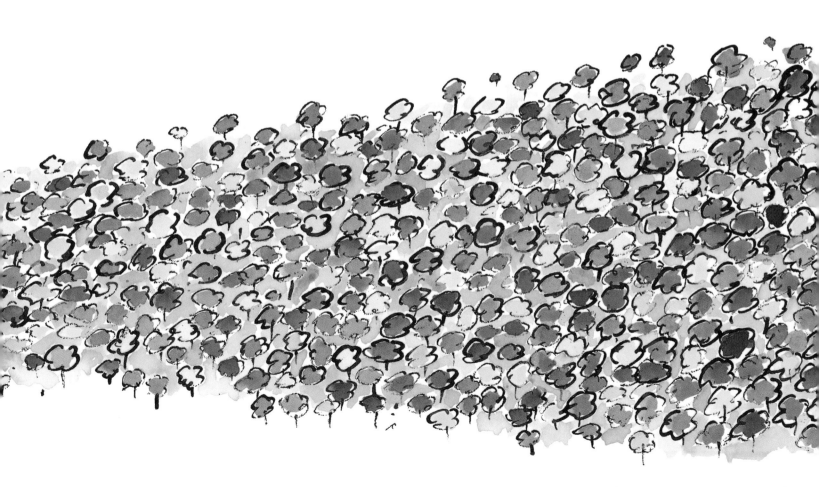

Hello,

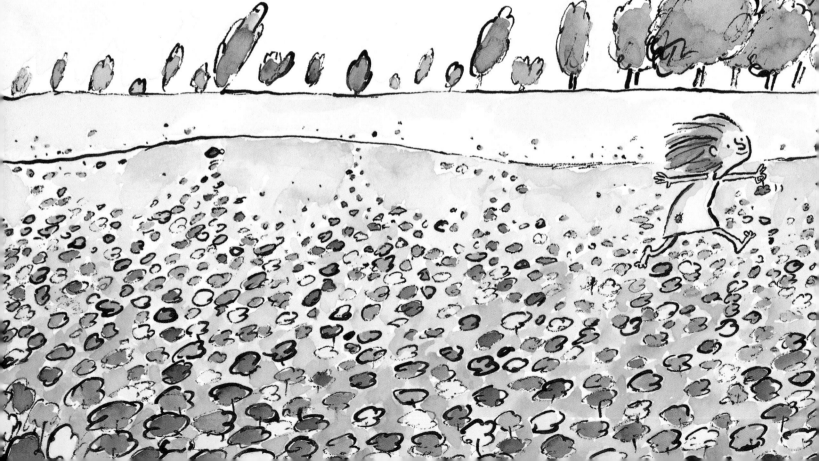

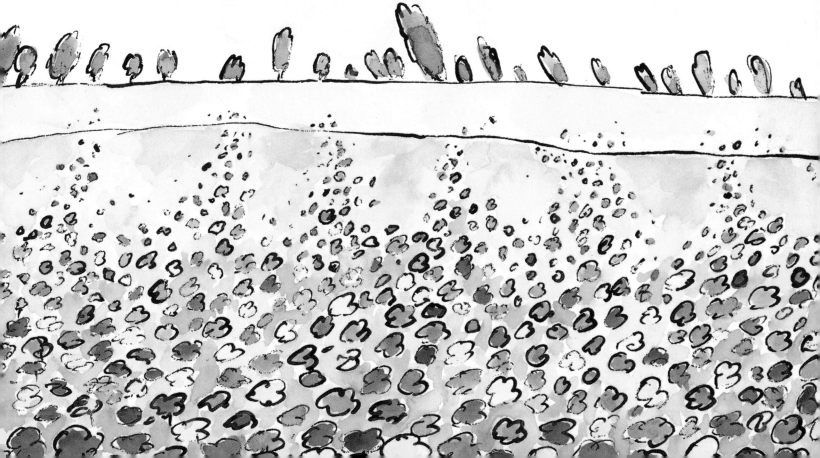

Hello... horse?

Hello,

RING

RING

RING

Hello?

HELLO ?!

Hello... *hello!*

Printed in Singapore
First edition
1 3 5 7 9 10 8 6 4 2
F850-6835-5-12166

The illustrations in this book were created with a bamboo pen and India ink,
a bit of pencil, a Macintosh computer, a large format waterproof inkjet printer,
and watercolor on paper.

Library of Congress Cataloging-in-Publication Data
Cordell, Matthew, 1975-
hello! hello! / Matthew Cordell.—1st ed.
p. cm.
Summary: A child seeks a way to communicate with parents and a brother
who are busy with their electronic devices.
ISBN 978-1-4231-5906-3
[1. Communication—Fiction. 2. Family life—Fiction.] I. Title.
PZ7.C815343Hel 2012
[E]—dc23   2011035439

Reinforced binding

Visit www.disneyhyperionbooks.com

Everything and always for
Julie and Romy